The Lion and the Mouse AND The Boy Who Cried Wolf

Text adapted by Amelia Marshall

Illustrated by Anni Axworthy
& Dan Howarth

W
FRANKLIN WATTS
LONDON • SYDNEY

The Lion
and the
Mouse

Illustrated by Anni Axworthy

Lion was asleep.
Mouse ran over Lion's
nose, waking him up!

Squeak!

Little Mouse felt brave.

Stop, Lion! I may help you one day.

Ha, ha! What a funny mouse! I will let you go.

Later that day,
Lion got stuck!

Day turned to night.
Lion was still stuck.

Now Mouse and Lion are
the best of friends!

Puzzle

Who says it? Match the characters with their speech bubbles.

1. 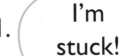 I'm stuck!

2. I may help you one day.

3. Squeak!

4. I will let you go.

5. Can you help?

6. I don't want to be eaten!

Story Quiz

1. What does Mouse do to Lion at the beginning of the story?

2. Why does Lion let Mouse go?

3. What happens to Lion?

4. How does Mouse help?

5. What happens to Mouse and Lion in the end?

The Boy
who cried
Wolf

Illustrated by Dan Howarth

There once was a shepherd boy who felt very bored.

I can make my own fun!

Help! Wolf!

The villagers came running!

We're coming!

14

The villagers were not happy.

But the boy was soon bored again.

Wolf! Hurry! Wolf!

The villagers ran to help.

Now the villagers were very cross.

18

And so the shepherd boy
lost all his sheep.

Puzzle

Who says it? Match the characters with their speech bubbles.

1. Not this time!

2. I can make my own fun.

3. Help! Wolf!

4. We're coming!

5. We'll save you!

6. Ha, ha tricked you!

Story Quiz

1. Why does the boy play a trick on the villagers?

2. What does he pretend is happening?

3. How many times does he play the same trick?

4. What happens when a wolf appears?

5. How does the boy feel at the end of the story?

Answers

The Lion and the Mouse

Puzzle (page 10)
Lion: 1, 4, 5
Mouse: 2, 3, 6

Story Quiz (page 11)
1. Wakes Lion up
2. Mouse makes Lion laugh
3. Lion gets stuck in a net
4. Mouse bites through the net
5. They become best friends

The Boy who cried Wolf

Puzzle (page 20)
Shepherd boy: 2, 3, 6
Villagers: 1, 4, 5

Story Quiz (page 21)
1. Because he is bored
2. He pretends he has seen a wolf
3. Twice
4. The villagers don't believe him
5. Sad, as he has lost his sheep

Franklin Watts

First published in Great Britain in 2016 by
The Watts Publishing Group

Text © Franklin Watts 2016
Illustrations for The Lion and the Mouse © Anni Axworthy 2009
Illustrations for The Boy Who Cried Wolf © Dan Howarth 2009

The rights of Amelia Marshall to be identified as the author and Anni Axworthy
and Dan Howarth as the illustrators of this Work have been asserted in accordance
with the Copyright, Designs and Patents Act, 1988.

Series Editor: Melanie Palmer
Series Designer: Peter Scoulding

A CIP catalogue record for this book is available
from the British Library.

ISBN 978 14451 4752 9 (hbk)
ISBN 978 14451 4754 3 (pbk)
ISBN 978 14451 4753 6 (library ebook)

Printed in China

Franklin Watts
An imprint of
Hachette Children's Group
Part of The Watts Publishing Group
Carmelite House
50 Victoria Embankment
London EC4Y 0DZ

An Hachette UK company.
www.hachette.co.uk

www.franklinwatts.co.uk

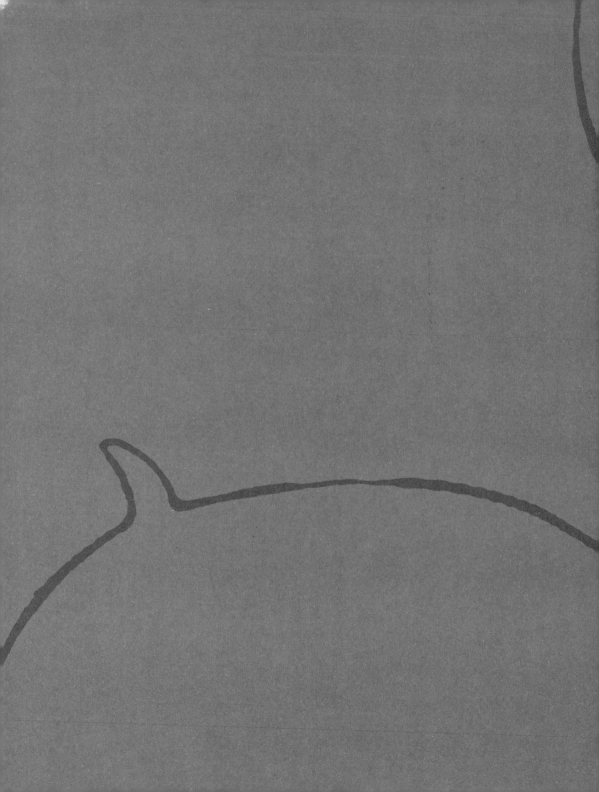